# This sub's for You

## An Erotic Collection of Short Stories

A Temptation Press Anthology

# This sub's for You

An
Erotic
Collection
of Short Stories

A Temptation Press'
Anthology

For permission requests, write to the publisher:
"Attention: Permissions Coordinator"
Temptation Press
PO Box 1172
Union Lake, Michigan 48387
mail to: info@TemptationPress.com

© 2018 Temptation Press – An Imprint of Zimbell House Publishing
Published in the United States by Temptation Press

This book is rated for 18+



Trade Paper ISBN: 978-1-947210-91-2
.mobi ISBN: 978-1-947210-92-9
ePub ISBN: 978-1-947210-93-6
Library of Congress Control Number: 2018911534

First Edition: October/2018
10 9 8 7 6 5 4 3 2 1

TEMPTATION
PRESS

## *Acknowledgments*

Temptation Press would like to thank all those that contributed to this anthology. We chose to showcase two new voices that best represented our vision for this work.

We would also like to thank all those on our Temptation Press team for all their hard work and dedication to these projects.

# Contents

**Asher's Dinner Party**                1

Gina Durden

**Switching**                15

Adeline Fox

**The Apothecary**                43

Gina Durden

**The Longer We Wait**                61

Adeline Fox

**Contributors**

**Other Works from Temptation Press**

**A Note from the Publisher**

# Asher's Dinner Party

Gina Durden

My slave came to me by accident. He walked up to me at a birthday party for an acquaintance and said, "Hello Miss," and we started talking.

He made it clear that he was interested only in service to a Mistress. I confessed right away that I knew nothing about being a Mistress, and he was understanding, as a slave should be, waiting for me to respond, not pushing.

As we talked, I found myself wanting to tell him what to do. I began by telling him to sit with me, which he did immediately and without question. His presence generated a small charge of energy in my lower abdomen, a sure sign that my body was interested. I mean, how often do you get an opportunity like this? The birthday girl had attracted a group of young men around her, and we were left chatting alone. She didn't need me.

How easy it was to take on the Mistress role. We totally ignored the rest of the party as I led him into the basement of my friend's house, had him kneel before me and show me how well he could pleasure a woman.

To make it harder, I told him he should remove my panties without the use of his hands. Kneeling before me, he pushed his head up under my skirt. His willing sweet lips and hot tongue did their precious duty, his teeth dragging at my undies. Sensing them ride half-on and half-off my buttocks sent shivers down my legs bringing more and more excitement to us both. Soon I was naked under my skirt, and his mouth went to work. With the merest nudge, I fell back onto the sofa and spread my legs to receive his head between them.

Spontaneously, I felt how wonderful it would be to delay him, and myself. As I experimented with pauses and rejections, we both were teased into deeper and deeper desire, and finally explosive release.

I was not ready to become a full Mistress, however, and thanked him for his service.

It was only a week or so before I encountered him again at a coffee shop in the area where we both lived. This time I approached him. Our second session involved a long massage and an afternoon in my hot tub, fully as satisfying as the first time.

The pleasure of having a willing handsome man do your bidding was beginning to grow on me. But was I ready to match his willingness to serve with a commitment to dominate him? I began to study the art.

A Mistress must be responsible for the care of her slave, not just his use. Though she may bind or taunt him, she must also tend, praise and reward him. If she is merciless, it should be to the end that both will be pleased. She must know what that means for herself and for him. She can rely on him to obey within limits they decide, but not necessarily to anticipate her needs. Perhaps anticipation could be taught. Already my mind was taking on the role.

I scanned the darker side of slavery. No, I would not inflict hard pain. I would not scar or injure him. I would not cage him and ignore him. I would be a merciful Mistress, and he would long for my force, knowing how well it would end for us both. Such service should be rewarded well, and I had come to believe that

Asher was truly desirous of absolute devotion to one woman. I studied the art of the Domme for weeks before feeling even remotely adequate.

The next time I saw him, I offered a trial run.

"If you agree, you will spend the week with me, Asher. After work every day you will come immediately to my place. There is a key under the statue in the hallway. You will undress, kneel inside the entrance and wait for me."

"Yes, Miss," he replied. "I am honored." And he let show a very brief, small smile.

Coming home every evening to find Asher waiting was a thrill. I found myself eager for the sight of him kneeling there, his hands on his hard thighs, his eyes downcast. I never knew how long he had been sitting there waiting for me to arrive. I had to clamp down on my sympathy, but I tried to arrive home quickly so that he was not put to too much waiting. Besides, being in my small apartment was so much more fun with Asher there.

Finding him away doing overtime or some necessary chore was always a disappointment. I would wait with anticipation for the door to open, and for Asher to step quietly inside and assume the position.

My first task was to whip him into shape. I enrolled him in a Martial Arts school and put him on a restricted, but healthy diet. He would quickly shed that extra bit of body fat. My slave would be the envy of all the women who saw us. Their jealousy would charge our passion, fusing our bond.

Our first month together we experimented with bondage. I practiced tying him in different positions and making him wait for me while I did other things, teasing him occasionally to keep him turned on and hungry for me.

I once placed him overnight, bound, in the corner of the bedroom, watching while I touched and teased myself, teasing him as well periodically, long into the night until we finally both fell fitfully asleep. I woke him early in the morning, untied and massaged him. Then I made him eat me, and then fuck me until we were both exhausted. We slept together like children until the afternoon, legs and arms sweaty and tangled.

That day we negotiated and committed for another month.

The sight of Asher bound began to work its power on me. I would look at that incredible body and think how it belonged to me and I could use it in any way I wanted. I would dream of ways to have him and wake thinking of more ways. He was my massuer, my servant, my helper, my friend, my lover. He was my own arms and hands and feet. He would hold me close and read to me until I fell asleep. I would wake with him asleep beside me, his head resting on my shoulder or in my lap. He was becoming an extension of myself, and he seemed to have endless endurance.

We talked at length about how he responded to pain. We experimented with pain. This was the hardest for me. I had come to love the growing dependencies between us and to inflict pain at first seemed impossible. We began with spanking, progressed to various whips and paddles, and stopped at caning. We studied the places on the body where pain could be inflicted without harm. I asked him to return the pain to me, and I found what my limits were as well.

I came to understand that the combination of sexual arousal with pain held an entirely new wonder, a place in the awareness that had no precedent in all my sexual experience. With the addition of pain, the senses become heightened. By alternating the stimulus of pleasure and pain, anticipation is increased both as avoidance and as desire. I could stroke and suck him until he was near ejaculating, then spank his bound body until he was near tears. Repeat. Repeat. Until both of us were roused to near exhaustion or release, and then fuck until we nearly passed out or came.

If you think that our life was one long tease, you would be mistaken. The more comfortable we became with each other; the more ordinary many aspects of life became.

We enjoyed the preparation of dinner together. We worked the Sunday crossword, at which Asher was no slacker or novice. We read books, both erudite and comical. We laughed together. We celebrated the holidays with friends and attended parties as lovers, though there was, more often than not, a secret bond of some kind between us. He might be bound under his clothes. There might be a slave collar under his turtleneck. Or clamps that he could not detach without my help.

Occasionally we would switch, and he would control some vibrator or device that would give me a little shock or titillation in public.

The occasion of Asher's birthday had been gathering attention in my mind. It coincided closely with our one-year anniversary. He would never have mentioned either of these events. If I forgot them, they would pass by unnoticed. But that is not the way of a good Domme.

A party began to form in my mind, a dinner at which Asher would be both the feaster and the feast. Two days before the dinner, I falsely accused Asher of some misdemeanor. I insisted that he be bound in the upstairs bathroom for a few hours. He acquiesced with only a little hesitation. Clearly, this was not my usual behavior. He had access to the toilet and the sink, so there was water available, and he would not suffer too much. He did not know that he would be up there for two days. I had to bite my nails to keep from letting him go, but without this preface, the dinner would not be as effective.

Asher had to trust me implicitly.

On the day of the dinner, I laid a long tarp under the dining room table. Our connection with a local BDSM group had allowed us to meet and enjoy others who loved the world of our unusual pleasures. I invited four nubile young women from among our BDSM friends to help me. I hired one of the young men to be a server and had all the food catered. I'm sure the caterer thought I was mad, but the food choice was critical as well as the order of service.

On the night of the party, I released him and showered with him and brought us both downstairs, naked, to the dinner table. He was savvy enough, and maybe a little wary of his new circumstances, to be silent, as I was silent. I had him assume the kneeling position on the floor on my right side and dinner began.

Seated two on each side of the table were the young women, also naked, as was the server. But since I wanted Asher's lovely cock to be the only one visible, the server wore a small apron. I used a cloth napkin to tie Asher's hands behind his back.

The first course was shrimp cocktail. We ladies devoured the serving with gusto, smacking our lips and putting on a great gush over the quality, lingering over the delicate pink curls of flesh and licking our fingers with a slurping noise. After two days without food, Asher must have been ravenous.

I looked down at him. I thought he might be drooling a bit. His eyes were glued on the shrimp I held in my hand, I dipped it in sauce and held it before him. He looked rather pleadingly at me and quickly back down.

He was so good, my boy.

I slipped a large shrimp between my first and second toes. Then another and another until my toes were laden with fleshy pink goodness and drenched with tart red sauce.

I nodded at Asher. His mouth opened and he swooped down on my foot, ravenous for the food. In no time, the shrimp was gone, and I felt the lovely sensation of Asher's tongue delicately licking and sucking every drop of sauce from my foot. He finished and smiled up at me, red sauce stuck around his mouth. I deftly cleaned his face with my napkin and called for the second course.

The soup was a light bisque of tomato, cream, and spices. I finished my own and asked for a second bowl. I dipped the other foot into the bowl and passed it to Asher. He cleaned it thoroughly several times. My feet were enjoying the meal as much as my mouth.

Next came the salad, quarters of delicate romaine slathered lightly with a tartly sweet vinaigrette. I stretched out my legs, closed them and trapped two quarters between my calves. To reach them Asher had to crawl under the table and settle himself over my legs. I felt his growing penis grazing my feet, as he well knew I had hoped.

The fourth course, a chicken and vegetable casserole required some finesse. Juicy and savory, the casserole would not stick to nor could not be held anywhere on my body. I closed my legs making a crevice and ladled spoonfuls of it between my thighs.

Of course, it was up to Asher to figure out how to acquire his next course from my body. Never one to be shy, he nuzzled his mouth between my thighs and began to lap unceremoniously at the chicken dish. All the remaining juices and pieces were readily disposed of by my very neat boy as I opened my legs to give him access to the last savory morsel.

The fifth course, a sherbet, would cleanse the palate. I covered his eyes with one of the cloth napkins so he would not know what was coming and fed him spoonfuls—cold, tart, and lemony—from my own dish. Watching his mouth open and waiting, so perfectly dependent on my care, moved me so deeply that tears came into my eyes, but a Domme should not allow this emotion to be evident in public. I would share it with Asher later.

I was sure Asher's appetite for food had been assuaged. But not his appetite for me. I think he must have smelled the next course, as he began to smile shyly.

Buttery herbed oysters lay in a ring around my plate. The young women were already anticipating my plan as they fingered their own oysters, no doubt wishing they had a slave to help them with theirs. I lifted the first oyster, spread my legs wide, slid down and forward on my seat, slipped the juicy oyster between the lips of my cunt and awaited Asher's approach.

Who was the Master here, and who the slave?

He knew what I wanted from him and did not disappoint. He began with a slow approach, not taking it eagerly in one gulp but licking and sipping at the juices before drawing it slowly from between my lips. The second oyster was treated the same. My own juices were blending with the salty, fishy sweetness, and Asher was lapping them up as well.

I dared to place the third one deeper. Asher responded with a slurping sucking action that the young girls could hear. They tittered over their plates and smiled at each other. I had to wipe the grin off my own face lest I join them in inappropriate silliness. I smeared the oyster juice up onto my clit, trapping the meat further north and hoping for a clit tease.

I was well rewarded.

All seven oysters went by way of Asher's hot mouth and tongue and down his throat. I was charged. My lips were swollen and salty. My clit was hard. I was panting, and I had to slow down because there was still desert.

I signaled the server, and he removed all the plates, leaving only the tablecloth. Now it was Asher's turn. I stood, extended my hand and lifted him from the floor. The napkin slid easily from his hands, as it was only a token binding after all.

"You are the dessert, my love," I said. "Climb on the table and be eaten."

He obliged me and lay down spread eagle on the table. At each of his hands and feet stood a lovely, naked young woman.

According to my plan, they each began to slather his arms and legs with chocolate ganache and went to work licking and slurping. As they worked, they also began to use his hands and feet to pleasure themselves. Working their hot cunts with his fingers and toes, and then pricking his limbs with the sharp point of a burr, stinging and pinching as only our kind know how.

I climbed on the table to give him my gift.

First, I slathered his cock with whipped cream and began to eat until my own face was dotted with white, nuzzling my mouth into his groin and licking everywhere—his balls, his thighs, his beautiful cock, and sucking on it until he began to stiffen quite proudly.

I pulled away and taking a sauce of hot chocolate from the server that had been heated to just the exact temperature to shock and not blister, drenched his belly with it and began again at his cock. Once he was about to peak again, I stopped, gave him a moment to recoup–he knew what I was doing–and went to his chest.

Taking spoonfuls of sweet raspberry ice in my mouth I slid the icy concoction along his sternum and throat, ending at his lips where I fed him like a mother bird the juice of my mouth mixed with icy raspberry. With my mouth now cool from the ice, I went back to work on his cock, shocking it a bit with the coldness, but quickly warming it up from the friction, I brought him to the peak again.

Again, I stopped.

There is a very refined art of stopping and starting such teasing. Knowing the exact moment to finalize the pleasure is crucial.

Asher's signal was when he began to roll his eyes back up into his head.

As he was peaking this time, I climbed on top of him and settled my cunt over his cock, with the head just barely inside. I watched his face. He looked at me briefly and nodded, a smile emerging slowly across his face.

"Happy birthday, Love," I said as I slid slowly down his shaft. Drawing back, I slid down again, even deeper. "And happy anniversary." The third time he was so ready, he exploded into me, shivering and pulsing.

I gave him all I had as well, there among the chocolate and whipped cream, the lingering tastes of oysters and raspberries, amid the pleasure and pain of our unique love.

# Switching

Adeline Fox

I made my first massage appointment the day that I was fired. It was not the most fiscally responsible reaction, but I knew that I could sooner fix my back pain than my life.

I could tell I was getting fired as soon as I walked in the door, only ten minutes late this time. Behind the counter, I saw Julia, who did not normally work on Tuesdays. James, my manager, stood beside her, writing the day's to-do list, looking pained. In the overstuffed back office, with the door ajar because it could never fully shut, James told me that this was the hardest time he'd ever had firing anyone. Since he'd worked more than fifty years as a manager, this was a bold statement and a small consolation for me.

James was a friend and father figure, at the age of sixty-four. He told me early on that he was in recovery, after I opened up to him about my own struggles. We were outside on a beautiful day, breaking down boxes and throwing them in the large green dumpster in the back parking lot. This was mostly an excuse for us to get outside. But for me, it was also a bonding moment, my manager opening up to me while breaking down boxes, a lowly task which he really didn't have to do. That's what made James such a good manager. No task was beneath him. He worked the register, folded clothes, even cleaned bathrooms.

"I've been a friend of Bill's for ten years today," he said, "Do you know what that means?"

I didn't. I lifted my stack of newly flattened cardboard and tossed it into the trash as James explained that today was his ten-year sober anniversary. We celebrated by lingering in the sun a while outside the store. There weren't any customers anyway. There were virtually never any customers. That's why I felt so devastated when he let me go. This was the perfect job for me—a retail job with no customers.

I became a friend of Bill's a week after James fired me. But first I walked around the cemetery behind the parking lot, pacing and crying, feeling suddenly cold even as the summer sun pounded down on my exposed limbs. When I got home and collapsed on my couch, I thought about finally finding a therapist. I rifled through my wallet for the business card of a therapist who'd been recommended to me, but instead, I came across a forgotten gift card to Healing Body Works, a gift from my ex. I called that number instead, making a massage appointment for the following day.

As I entered the small waiting room of the spa the next morning, my head was pounding, and I felt empty. I hadn't been able to eat anything. I felt indifferent toward food. I checked in with a cheery receptionist and sat down to wait. Water trickled through a fountain. Underneath the sound of easy listening music, I could just barely make out another sound—a noise machine—adding a subtle, serene layer to the scene by blocking out the noise from outside.

"Lily?"

I heard a gentle male voice calling my name and looked up to see him gesturing down the hall with a smile. I gathered my heavy bag up off the floor. It was full of copies of my resume, and my computer. I told myself I'd fill out applications while I was downtown, but I ended up running late looking for parking, and now the weight of my future was doing nothing but worsen my back pain.

"I'm Christopher," he said as we walked down the hallway toward his office's open door. Inside, I was met with the scent of jasmine and vanilla. Soft, atmospheric music piped in from overhead speakers.

There were crystals everywhere, mostly amethyst and quartz. I learned to identify some crystals at the shop, where we sold small stones for seventy-five cents. The stones came with little cards promising qualities such as strength, stability, calm, reserve, or joy. Each stone had a specialty, its own coveted quality.

All for less than a dollar. The memory made me sad.

"So, what brings you here?" Christopher asked. He was holding a clipboard with the form I'd filled out in the waiting room. He stood leaning against the edge of the massage table.

"Lower back pain," I answered. "Everything else is fine."

"No chronic health issues?" He asked. He gave my form a once-over, then looked me in the eyes for a response. After I answered that I had none, he neatly placed the clipboard on a side table. I noticed his trimmed, dark beard and bright smile. He looked relaxed and genuinely happy to be at work. He asked me if I'd ever had a massage before, and what level of pressure I needed.

"A lot," I said. My hands instinctively shot to the area in my lower back that was a constant, tight knot. "I'm trying to fix my back. I don't even really need it to feel good today ... I'd just like it to hurt less in the future."

"Gotcha. Well hopefully we should be able to do both ... make you feel better today and get some of the kinks out. But I don't want to go so hard that you're sore tomorrow."

My mind wandered in a dirty direction, and I realized how long it had been since I'd been touched by anyone.

"I've got the table warmer on," he continued, patting the table behind him, "but I can turn it off. Let me know if you want me to adjust the music, the temperature, the pressure. Please tell me if anything is bother-ing you."

I felt inexplicably nervous when he showed me the brown wicker box where I was to place my clothes and jewelry. He said he'd give me a few minutes to get settled and then he'd knock on the door. I nodded, unsure what to say. After I heard the door click behind me, I quickly stood up, slipped my dress off and into the box, removed my underwear and plucked off my earrings, placing it all into the wicker box and shutting it.

I lifted the top sheet on the massage table, unsure if I should lay face-up or face-down. I opted for face-down, placing my face in the headrest, staring down at grey carpet and trying to relax, to forget, but my mind wandered to my worries; to my lack of employment, to my drinking which was likely the cause, and even distantly to the ex-boyfriend who gifted me this massage nearly a year ago now. I felt so lonely I could cry.

I heard a soft knock on the door and Christopher's voice asking, "Are you all set?"

I lifted my head up out of the rest, making sure he'd hear me say yes.

I could feel the man's presence in front of me. I thought I wouldn't like having a male massage therapist. When I called to book my appointment, there was no one else available. As it turned out, Christopher's calm demeanor was contagious and helped me relax. I trusted him completely, immediately.

His voice was hypnotizing.

"Thank you, Lily, for being my guest," he said. "And if you'd like, I invite you to begin with some deep, relaxing breaths. Carve out some space here for yourself."

I heard Christopher take a deep breath himself, and I mimicked, letting air fill my chest and lift me slightly toward his hands as they contacted my shoulder blades.

Warmth spread through me as if Christopher's hands were a beam of light. Lavender filled my nostrils, and the soothing classical music helped take my mind off of things, but it was Christopher's soft, firm hands, coated in massage oil, which eased my mind through my body. I didn't know a stranger could do that to me.

I felt waves of arousal throughout the session. I felt like I shouldn't let my mind drift in a sexual direction, that somehow, he could tell, but as his hands moved up and down my entire body, into all of the tight and knotted places that I couldn't reach myself, I thought of his sweet smile. I wondered what his life was like outside of work. I wondered what he was like sexually, if he was as focused on his partners' pleasure in bed as he was with his clients at work.

I couldn't believe how fast the massage went by. That morning, waking up to the recollection that I'd been fired, the hours had dragged on and on. But before I knew it, Christopher was resting his hands on my back and saying, "Thank you. I'll step out now. Just poke your head out when you're dressed. Take your time."

Pulling my dress back on over my now oil-coated skin, I felt fuzzy-headed, dazed, and a little dizzy. As instructed, I poked my head out the door, and heard Christopher's chipper voice say, "Hey! How do you feel?" as he re-entered the room.

"Good," I said. "Better."

"Great!" He said. "Do you want to book another?"

The question caught me off guard. My pleasant fuzzy-headedness, combined with the renewed feeling of vitality throughout my body, made me want to say yes. This wasn't supposed to be a regular occurrence. But I couldn't help myself. I booked another appointment and told myself that by the next time I saw Christopher, I would have a job.

After booking, he told me to drink lots of water and wished me a happy rest of my day. I reluctantly left his world of lavender and soft music, venturing back to bright, unemployed reality.

The next time I saw Christopher, I still did not have a job, but I did have a scheduled interview, and that was something. The interview was for another retail job, in a toy store. Working there would surely be less fun than my previous job. But maybe the noise of screaming children would help motivate me to avoid the headaches associated with drinking.

Christopher greeted me in the waiting room as if he were running into an old friend. His smile lit up his face. I couldn't help but smile back as I followed him down the hall to his sanctuary of relaxation. He asked if anything were new with my body. I told him no.

When he thanked me for 'being his guest' and invited me to take a deep breath, I once again experienced the power of this seemingly simple action. His hands rubbed circles around my shoulders. His elbows found knots I didn't realize were there until I felt the tension releasing from them under his weight. He moved down to my lower back, finding the painful spots which had not subsided even though I hadn't been doing any heavy lifting since losing my job. After rubbing every inch of me down to my feet, he pulled my legs toward him, lengthening me and straightening my spine. I felt my body respond in thankful, healing pleasure.

Sometimes, the pressure of his hands on my lower back, pushing my naked body toward the massage table, stimulated my clit, and I had to take a long, slow breath to handle the sensation.

I let my mind wander to sexual fantasies of this man. He'd never have to know; it did him no harm for me to picture him naked and under my control. I wondered, hoped against all reasonable hope that he was as submissive and accommodating as a lover as he was when giving massages.

Of course, I'd never have the opportunity to find out.

It would be completely inappropriate to ask him out.

This was a professional relationship.

I repeated the word over and over in my head, *professional.* But his hands were still forcing me against the table, my breaths still coming slow and labored.

By the time the massage was over, and Christopher left the room for me to dress, I was so horny I felt tempted to touch myself right there. I knew it would only take seconds for me to orgasm.

Of course, I couldn't do that.

The very thought was embarrassing. I took a deep breath and a vow to never come back to this place. It was too much.

I felt flustered when he re-entered the room. We chatted for nearly fifteen minutes, just making small talk, even after I declined to book another appointment. I kept looking at the clock, wondering if he realized how much time had passed.

He assured me that I was his last appointment of the day.

Still, I felt like I must have been holding him up from heading home, so I stood up to leave. I may have been imagining it, but he looked sad to see me go.

James accompanied me to my first AA meeting. I had been sober a few weeks before I let him know. Of course, he was happy for me, thrilled, but it was still difficult to bring up. I knew he'd want me to go to meetings, and I wasn't sure I could do it.

"Don't be nervous," he said as we pulled into the church parking lot.

I laughed. "Impossible."

"Well, I know how you feel," he said.

Inside, we drank the worst coffee I'd ever had, out of mismatched mugs with spiritual quotes on them. James spotted me reading my mug.

"You don't have to believe any of the religious stuff if you don't want to," he said. "This is about finding a community."

I looked around, unsure that I wanted to trade my friends for these strangers, trade nights at the bar for nights drinking bad coffee in folding chairs in a church basement.

James and I took our seats toward the back stairwell. He asked me about my job search and reminded me that he'd give me a glowing recommendation.

A clock on the cement wall behind the stage clicked loudly. I felt relieved by the commotion of bodies moving toward the seats and the sudden presence of a heavyset fifty-something man with a bushy grey beard now in front of the group. He gave a brief welcome, some announcements, then read the twelve steps and the twelve traditions.

A woman who had been sober for fifteen years walked up next, her heels clicking against the tiled floor. She gave an abbreviated version of her rock-bottom story, which involved waking up in her car in the middle of the woods. Then she talked about her current struggle. She said at this stage it wasn't the summer barbeques or open-bar weddings that tempted her, it was boredom most of all that sent her staring into the windows of liquor stores on her walk home from work.

That did not make me feel better.

Nothing anyone said made me feel a shred better.

My mug of bad coffee was now empty. My grumbling stomach reminded me that I'd skipped dinner.

The meeting soon ended. James insisted that I talk to at least one person before he would drive me home. Then he abandoned me at the coffee station. I watched him walk across the room and shake hands with the man who made the opening statements.

I briefly considered just leaving, letting James find me outside, but I was sure to find just as many attendees on the church steps smoking cigarettes and chatting there, too.

"Lily?" I heard from behind me. The voice broke me out of my scheming.

I turned to see the smiling face of Christopher, my massage therapist. I hadn't seen him in weeks. He looked so out of place here. Standing a foot away from me, he still smelled faintly of vanilla and massage oil. He radiated calm.

"Hi," I said back, probably betraying the surprise in my tone.

"First time?" he asked.

"Huh?"

"First meeting?" he clarified.

"Oh, yeah," I said, refilling my coffee mug although it was nearly full already.

"You've got the look," he said. Then he leaned toward me to quietly say, "I know how you feel."

I was getting tired of hearing that.

He paused. His green eyes ventured up to the ceiling, thinking. He added, "No one ever regrets getting sober."

"Can we ..." I said, "Talk about something else?"

"Sure," he answered. "Of course."

"Well ... what do you do besides giving massages and not drinking?"

We had made quite a bit of small talk at my last appointment but hadn't covered hobbies.

I wrapped my arms around my body, probably looking standoffish when I was really just cold. Christopher stood in a relaxed posture, one arm grabbing the other by the elbow behind his back. My eye caught his toned muscles and spotted a tattoo of a bird on his left wrist.

"I like to go to the meditation center downtown. They have free sittings every Wednesday. And I like to eat out a fair amount too. It's indulgent ... but hey, you gotta eat, and I figure since I quit drinking ... Willpower, I've found, is a fixed resource. I'm liable to run out of it if I deny myself too much."

He smirked a little bit when he said that and my mind ventured in a dirty direction as it always did with him. I shook the thought away. I was reading too much into everything. My face must have flushed with nervousness.

"Do you have any good recommendations for restaurants within walking distance?" I asked. "I'm starving."

"Too many to name!" he said. "I'd be happy to take you for a walk and point them out."

"Oh … well, I got a ride here with a friend. I should find him now actually. It was nice talking to you."

Christopher looked disappointed as I walked over to James, who gave me a sly smile.

"What?" I asked. "No one should look as happy at one of these things as you do right now." The whole evening had left me emotionally drained, and I was fantasizing about eating ice cream in bed with the TV on.

"I see you met Christopher."

"Yeah, he's my massage therapist."

James clicked his tongue. "Lucky you," he said.

"Stop," I said, hitting his arm. I felt my cheeks grow hot again.

"Not only is he cute, but he's very nice, Lily."

"How do you even know he's into me?" I asked.

"I was watching. I know what flirting looks like. I've been doing it since before you were born."

"He did offer to take me on a walk, and maybe get dinner?"

"Go!" James responded, practically shoving me in Christopher's direction. "Before he leaves! Now listen," he put his hand on my arm, "I'm breaking all the rules, you know. You're really not supposed to get involved with anyone this early into sobriety. But Christopher … he's very stable. I mean anyone can relapse, you know that, but I don't think he will. And I know you two would get along. I've thought about this before actually."

I rolled my eyes.

"See I knew you wouldn't go for it if I suggested it, but look … the fates are on my side." James stood up straight and cocky. He read too many romance novels.

I looked around to where Christopher had been stacking chairs, but I didn't see him. My heart sank. I'd missed my chance. Finally, a cute guy wanted me, for the first time in a year, a guy who was James-approved, and I blew it. I was too ashamed to admit my defeat to James, so I decided I would just walk home, and find myself something to eat on the way. A slice of pizza, maybe.

Outside, the night air felt pleasant. The door shut loudly behind me. Walking down the church steps, I spotted Christopher, unlocking his sleek black car. I quickened my pace but tried not to appear like I was running toward him.

"Christopher!" I called out, a little too loudly.

He looked up and smiled.

"Actually, change of plans ... I'm free," I blurted out. "If you still want to—"

"Definitely," he said. "Let me just lock my stuff up in the car."

I watched him slide a speaker and microphone into the backseat. "Those are yours?" I asked, stating the obvious, wondering why he had a microphone.

"Yup. I play guitar and sometimes perform. It's good to have your own mic, just in case, you know? Venues can be unreliable. Plus, I lend my mic to the meetings, and it keeps me accountable. Can never miss one."

We made our way through the empty parking lot, down a hill, to Main Street. Powerful gusts of occasional wind gave the summer night a stormy, ominous feeling. The sky was clear of clouds and brightened by the moon, but the lights of downtown obscured the stars.

Christopher caught me looking up, and he looked up too. Although there were no stars in the murky black above us, his thoughts had turned skyward. He asked me my 'sign.'

"I'm a Leo," I said, a hint of mockery in my voice indicating that I don't think much of astrology.

"Wow, I never would have guessed," he said.

"Why not?"

"They tend to be ... dramatic," his eyes widened.

"Well. You don't know me very well yet," I said.

"You're right I guess, I don't. Yet," he said.

Each time we passed a restaurant he gave me the run-down of the food they served and the atmosphere. By the time we walked past the third place, I told him I was too starved for decision making and that we should just eat there.

I rolled my eyes when he explained that he was into food and other 'sensual pleasures' because he was a Taurus.

The walls of India Palace had been painted with vibrant colors—blood orange and maroon. The lone server seated us in a cozy booth by the window, swiftly bringing over a pitcher of water and an appetizer of naan with three different sauces.

With some bread in my stomach, I could think clearly enough to choose an entree, deciding on the lamb with curried rice and vegetables. I relaxed into the cushioned booth behind me, and my leg brushed against Christopher's. I practically jumped back, and he laughed.

"Am I that radioactive?" he asked.

"Not at all!" My heart pounded in my chest. I took a long drink of water. Ice clinked around in my glass.

"I noticed you haven't made an appointment in a while," he said.

"Yeah, about that. I don't think I can be your client anymore."

He looked genuinely hurt and confused. "Oh."

"It's not that—" I spat out, unsure how to begin, "you're a great massage therapist. Fantastic. You're too good. I mean."

"I'm too good?" he said, incredulous.

"You're too … attractive," I said, barely above a whisper.

"Too what?" he asked.

I couldn't tell if he actually hadn't heard me or if he just wanted to make me say it again. There was a playful teasing demeanor about him this evening. I didn't entirely mind.

"Attractive, okay, you're too cute."

"I didn't know that was a deal-breaker for clients," he joked.

"I just didn't think it was appropriate. For me to get massages when I have a … when I like you … It isn't really all that relaxing you know … it's kind of the opposite of relaxing."

He laughed. I thought I might die of embarrassment. *Why had I said that?*

The server brought over tremendous plates of food, and we paused the conversation until she left.

"I like you too, Lily. If you don't want to be my client anymore, that's probably a wise decision, because I would happily give you massages for free, if you'll let me."

He casually began eating his food and commenting on his meal, as if this were a perfectly normal conversation for him. I shook my leg up and down with nervous energy. I ate my lamb and veggies just to avoid having to speak. I kept waiting for the punchline, or to wake up from this strange dream.

After dinner, Christopher walked me to my apartment.

"This is me," I said at my steps, then turned around to thank him for dinner but he spoke first.

"May I kiss you?" he asked. It was such a comfortable question coming from him, from his sweet and familiar voice. This was the voice that asked me if the pressure was okay, if I liked the music, if I wanted the table warmer turned on or off.

"Yes," I said. His lips had the same effect on me as his adept hands did when he massaged my muscles. He felt soft and warm. His kiss was firmer than I expected. He placed a hand on my back to draw me closer. But like his massages, it was over too soon. He squeezed my hand, and we made plans for the weekend.

Christopher asked me out on a date the night after my first day at my new job. I felt like I might explode from the anxiety of work compounded with date jitters. But at least when he asked me how my day went, I'd have something to talk about. Plus, my first day of work went smoothly. My new boss, though she would certainly be no James, was kind and patient with me as I learned the routine.

Christopher asked if he could pick me up at six o'clock, which I thought was a tad on the early side, but if I were being honest with myself, I didn't want to wait another minute to see him. I wore my favorite yellow sundress and sandals. When he opened my door, I noticed that he was wearing hiking boots and jeans, but I didn't think anything of it. He'd wanted to surprise me with his evening plans.

When we pulled into the parking lot of the nature reserve, I was worried he wanted to hike the trails, which I couldn't do in my sandals. Instead, he lead me to a clearing just a few feet into the woods and set up a picnic.

"I like to come here in the evenings," he said, "and watch the sunset."

"With all of your many dates?" I asked. I imagined he could get laid as often as he cared to.

"By myself," he said.

"Oh," I responded, opening a seltzer, the classic drink for those who are both sober and health conscious but want something more exciting than water.

"I'm good company," he said. "I like to spend a lot of time with me."

"Well," I responded. "How can I compete?"

He leaned over and kissed me.

Time seemed to stop when I was with Christopher, whether we talked or didn't talk, touched or didn't touch. When the sun set several hours later, I could see why he made a habit of coming here for it. In the clearing, we could see as far as the surrounding mountains. The sky was tinged with pink. I took a deep breath and tried to feel grateful for this moment—something I'd been working on.

Back at my apartment, it was clear that Christopher wanted to come in, so I lead him into the living room, apologizing for the slight mess. He sat down on the couch. I kept walking to the kitchen but had nothing to offer him.

"Are you gonna sit down?" he asked, after watching me open and close several cabinets and pace around like an idiot.

"Yes. No."

"Hmm," he said. "Something wrong with the couch?"

"I don't know how to do this without alcohol," I blurted.

"Ah, I see," he said.

"Normally, with booze, you just sort of fall into each other and pick up the pieces where they land. I don't even know how to get you upstairs. My bed. It's upstairs. Here we are ... downstairs. I can't remember what happens in between. There's just—drinks."

"Lily?" he said. I looked up at him.

"Yeah?"

"Would you like to go upstairs?" he asked.

"Yes," I said. We both smiled.

He took the stairs to my bedroom two at a time.

Then I remembered the restraints that lay, permanent and unused for months now, at the edge of my bed. *How could I have forgotten?* Obviously, we were going to end up back here, and now he was going to think I was a freak. I bolted over and leaned against my bed in a futile attempt to hide the cuffs. I heard him laughing.

"What are you doing now?" He asked, putting his arms around me. "I know what those are." He kissed me behind the ear.

"Oh yeah?" I asked.

"They're kind of amateur," he said.

I scoffed.

"Have you ever used a spreader bar?" he asked. "I think they're much better."

"Of course, I have all that stuff in my closet. It's just nice to have these in a pinch."

"Fair enough," he said.

"Now, a moment of truth Christopher. Whose limbs are we restraining?"

He put his hands up in surrender. "Your call," he said. "I'm a switch."

"I'm a bit of a switch too," I admitted, "But mainly just a Dom."

This conversation perfectly segued into creating a safe word and establishing what we were and were not willing to do. Once that was covered, I shoved him onto my mattress.

Every other guy I'd slept with had been shocked to learn of my kinks. They seemed to think sexual dominance was antithetical to my nervous personality, but I think my sexual personality lives in perfect harmony with the rest of me.

Kink shuts off my brain. My animal brain takes over and tells me what to do, as I tell my sub what to do. I feel completely in control and not only do I get off on it, it's practically therapeutic. I don't have to second guess myself or worry about what to do.

In the absence of any play during the past year, I felt anxious and frazzled. Now, all of my anxiety about this budding relationship melted away as my inner Dom took over.

It felt amazing for Christopher to be the one laying down and responding to my touch, instead of the other way around like our massage sessions. Since he'd mocked the under-the-bed restraints, I got out the heavy-duty spreader bars instead, placing his delicate wrists and ankles into the cuffs.

The expression on his face changed instantly. He still looked his usual calm, accepting self, but I could detect excitement brewing.

Before I even touched him, Christopher's breathing grew rapid. He closed his eyes and furrowed his brow. I watched his cock grow hard.

"Touch me," he begged.

I laughed. "I ought to spank you for even asking."

Instead, I stripped my clothes off as he watched. He lay completely powerless, his eyes pleading. He strained against the cuffs, aching to touch and be touched. I sat on his thighs, as if I might touch his cock, then pretended like I'd changed my mind. But it was my plan all along to make him eat me out until I felt satisfied, only returning pleasure if I felt he'd done a sufficient job pleasing me. I'd been dreaming of this since my first massage.

His tongue found my clit immediately and stayed there. Unlike so many men I'd slept with he didn't try to impress me with too much variety. He knew what I needed. He put consistent pressure on my clit, at just the right rhythm. He moaned against me, and the vibration of his moaning mouth sent me over the edge.

Christopher was used to listening to my body. He was used to his body putting pressure on mine just where I needed it. We were completely in sync.

I felt he deserved a reward, and I enjoy sucking cock anyway, so I put him in my mouth just long enough where I felt he was close to orgasm. If his hands weren't restrained, I'm sure he'd be gripping my arms tightly in that silent gesture which says, "don't stop."

But I did stop. He practically whimpered.

"Please fuck me," he said quietly.

I made him say it louder and louder, making him really wonder if I ever would.

He exploded in thank yous when I placed a condom on him and rode him at my preferred pace. He wasn't afraid to show me his appreciation through sexy groans. I loved how loud he was. When I came, I clung to his tight body, and the whole world disappeared.

Life with Christopher fell into a rhythm immediately. We were soon spending every day together. During the day we'd wake up early and discuss our dreams over coffee. He drove me to work when the weather was bad. In the evening, we went to meetings. This meant that I still got to see James every week. He'd started talking about the possibility of buying the shop from the owners since they were getting tired of running it. I didn't let myself get my hopes up too much, but he assured me that given my improvement and sobriety, he would hire me back in a heartbeat if he ever bought the place.

It was the owners of the shop who had been unwilling to give me another chance. Second, third, and even fourth chances were a tenant of James' life philosophy. He'd been given his fair share and felt he owed it to the world to give back in the form of forgiveness and generosity. James, Christopher and I formed an odd little trio and spent a lot of time together before and after meetings. I think we all began to feel a lot less alone as a result of this arrangement. We could speak openly about our struggles with addiction, holding each other accountable and empathizing at the same time.

Christopher and I went out to eat frequently, or else he made me delicious dinners at home. In those moments when I doubted my ability to hold down my new job and my new sobriety, he gave me gentle massages which escalated quickly into foreplay and a variety of sexual play.

As a switch, he started to bring out my submissive side, on occasion. After several minutes of massaging, Christopher would inevitably get too aroused to continue, and then the switch fighting would start.

I never imagined a relationship could be so sexy.

When Christopher was in a dominant mood, he'd try to transition from massaging me to restraining me. But I wouldn't give in that easily. Switch fights, luckily, are a fight in which everyone wins. We would check in occasionally, outside of the bedroom, to make sure each of us got to play the dominant role enough for our individual needs. But most of the time, we were more than happy to wrestle rather than ask for the role of Dom.

Winning was intoxicating—managing to escape Christopher's grasp and pinning him to the mattress, then putting a collar on him to claim my victory. I loved teasing him, bringing him to the brink of orgasm several times in a row before letting him finish, making him ask me first and punishing him for any transgressions from the rules I set. I always made sure I came first.

Losing, though it happened less often, was sexy too. Struggling under his strong, adept muscles made the play feel so real, it was almost scary. I really had no choice, sometimes, which was absolutely freeing. He'd laugh once he got the collar and leash on me, dragging my neck down to his cock and forcing me to suck it, slapping my face if I tried to refuse. I liked refusing, enjoyed struggling as long as possible to make him more and more forceful. With my body bent over to suck his cock, he could easily whip my ass, reminding me of the power he held over me.

It was convenient to be able to keep all of our toys out in the open, within arm's reach in our bedroom. I didn't have to hide anything from Christopher. He wasn't intimidated by my array of vibrators. When he went through his dominant phases, he sometimes hid them, leaving mocking notes in their place and returning them to me only after he felt I'd been sufficiently good. A new side of me opened up. I wanted to please him as much as he pleased me. Never knowing which one of us would win a switch fight meant I was never, ever bored in bed.

My evenings with Christopher turned from sweet to sexy, and vice versa, on a dime. We were both as skilled at cuddling and aftercare as we were at dominating each other.

One evening, cuddling after a particularly long session in which he had primarily been the one in control, he confided in me that he'd had a crush on me since the day we met.

"It was so hard not to rip that sheet off you when you were my client," he whispered.

"Christopher!"

"It's true! Our first session, I was petrified that you would see that I was hard."

Under the guise of polite smiles and professional behavior, we had both been mentally undressing each other for weeks, fantasizing about the very things we ended up doing to one another on an almost daily basis.

But neither of us imagined that we'd also be building a comfortable life together—as sweet and predictable as our sex life was dirty and spontaneous.

# The Apothecary

*Gina Durden*

It seemed at first a coincidence that I was the one to find her notebooks. I was directing a team of paranormal researchers who had come in to clean up the dark, dingy place—part home, part apothecary, part storefront. The apothecary was filled with strange herbs and liquids, the walls a warren of shelves and cabinets, dusty now and in a shamble. The section called home was no more than a single large room on the upper floor with a kitchen and bath at one end and a bed at the other. Their bones had lain there for years before anyone suspected. On the door at the storefront an "out of business" sign dangled, hand-written and crooked.

Thought to be a witch's sanctuary, the building had to be cleared before new tenants could move in. My team was sent to do the job, physically and psychically. A thick dusty notebook had been secreted behind a false cabinet back.

In among the recipes and instructions were pages recapping years-long segments of her life. I wondered why she bothered to hide it. Who had she imagined might discover it? I opened the book, skipping the recipes, which meant nothing to me, and scanned the biographical sections.

Her hand was firm and sure if a bit eccentric. Leafing through the pages front to back, I discerned in the loops and serifs of her handwriting the emotions of youth, then her focused and confident middle age, turning toward the end to crooked, angry deterioration, and finally fewer and fewer entries. A few words captured my attention, enough that I could not immediately put the book down.

No chairs remained in the abandoned storefront, so I unbuttoned my coat and sat on the floor, even knowing my pants and jacket would be coated with dust. As I read her entries, I gradually became aware they were intended for me. She not only told her story, but mine as well. My imagination filled in the action as if it had happened to me.

Sensoria's Tale - Excerpts

## Youth

I am a plain girl. I know that this is true. Eyes do not follow me. Ears do not listen to me. Attention does not linger around me. Neither my body nor my voice attracts. My opinions never mattered to anyone but my grudging Aunt, who used me like a servant and a watchdog, taking the place of her aging eyes and ears.

She taught me well from the age of five to manage the store, to grind and stew, to brew and steep, to extract and combine. There is nothing I don't know of her ways, and some things I have discovered on my own.

She did not encourage me to seek a beau or a lover even after my breasts emerged and my flow began. Though I know that she had many in her long lifetime. The spells and potions she kept in her special hideaway have told me much about her liaisons with well-known gentlemen, their names or initials stuck to the bottom of the bottles.

I have pondered the usefulness of these potions and am determined that I will not have a lover made mine by magick. Still, the black hole that I am, empty of any love now that she is gone, sucks at the living with a greater passion than ever. Men and women, old and young, enter the shop for their cures and potions. I wrap and box and bottle of the magick that I know by heart. All the while, my eyes search for someone who sees me not merely as a Mistress of the Arts, but as a person. A woman.

For a while, I attempted to make myself lovely. I purchased nice clothes. I wore makeup. I tried every potion known to me and searched further through my Aunt's paraphernalia. Nothing, it seemed, could overcome the limp hair, the dull eyes, the thin lips and worst of all the piping voice that aired its inadequacies to the world day after day.

Eventually, I gave up trying and took comfort in my skills. I became a true practitioner not only of magick but of healing and seering. I found I had a talent for reading a person's aura and coming to know their maladies quickly.

What I lacked in admirers, I made up for in knowledge.

What I lacked in beaus, I made up for in self-sufficiency.

What I lacked in love, I made up for in power.

My piping voice grew into a richer alto. My hair was tamed and bound into a severe bun. My clothes took on the monochromatic colors of the dry earth. Dry as the powders I ground. As such, I reached my thirtieth year, lonely and unwed.

## Aiden

My seering seemed to work for everyone but myself. Although I had tried to see myself in the mirror the same as I did with customers, I only saw the face of a sad, dark woman.

My prediction for her—more sadness, more darkness.

The day that Aiden walked in I was not expecting anything. He had entered so quietly I might have missed him, if not for almost stumbling over him. I was on my way from the back room to the front to lock up when I glimpsed his dark form huddled by the door.

"Who are you? What are you doing hanging about here? You're obviously not a customer." I said. I had become a bit curt over time, you see, one might even say acerbic.

"Just waiting, miss. For you to notice."

He was squatting by the door almost as if trying to hide there. His clothes were not dirty but by no means well fitted or new. There was no color visible, and if a hint of color was there, it had long ago faded to something drab.

"Stand up," I told him. And he did.

He was not a small man, rather a few inches taller than me. His eyes downcast but graced by long dark lashes, his mouth full and well defined, his shape slim and lithe but not obviously muscular. He was no dock worker or farm laborer.

"Look at me," I said. "What do you want? I'm just closing up."

He lifted a pair of soft brown eyes to mine briefly and looked quickly back down. Something about him tugged at me. I defined it as pity at the time.

"Do you need help here? It would be an honor to help you, miss."

"Honor indeed," I laughed. "My honor to let you in my back room to rearrange the goods and put everything in the wrong place!"

"I would never, miss. I just want to help."

"Why? Why would you want to help me?"

"I was born because of your Aunt. My mother almost died when she was pregnant, and your Aunt's remedy helped her thrive and bear me. She lived a long life and bore others. Now she's dead. I tended her until she passed and now I need to find a job for myself."

Mercy was not in my emotional alphabet. I could not afford it. Yet once again, there was this tug.

"What can you do?"

"Sweep, clean up, put things away. You will show me what to do, and I will do it without fail, miss."

I hired him to start the next morning. He was prompt and tidy. Everything I told him was done with swiftness and accuracy. It was as if he had come out of the ether from some fairie land to ease my day and care for my shop. He swept, he cleaned, he ran errands, and he waited on customers when I was busy. He hung around until I closed every night and then went away, I knew not where. I did not ask. We passed a couple of months in this mode.

One cold stormy night I closed so late that I hated to send him out into the weather. I suggested he sleep in the storeroom.

"Come on then and have some supper." I invited him up into my room for the first time and settled him in the only chair, at the only table. He ate what I fed him and stood. "Your chair now, miss."

"Oh, I don't need that. My aching feet are filling my head with woe. I want most of all to lie down."

"I can help with that, miss. I used to rub my mother's feet. She said I was good at it."

I looked at him. He looked so innocent. *Well, I could protect myself from any man,* I affirmed silently, mainly for my own benefit. I knew Martial arts as well as the dark ones.

"Very well, let's see how well you do." I stretched out with my feet at the foot of the bed. "Pull up the chair and sit at my feet. Do your job, Aiden."

When I woke, not knowing how long I had slept, Aiden was still at my feet. It had become dark outside, the rain and wind had stopped, and moonlight was streaming in the east window. His hands were like the wings of birds on my feet. Still moving, still patiently stroking and caressing. I felt dreamy and half asleep.

"You can go now, Aiden," I said. "Thank you."

I slept the sleep of the rich that night and woke to a long pleasurable stretch. Breakfast was beside the bed. Aiden was at the kitchen table.

"You didn't have to do this," I said pointing to the plate of eggs and toast. "You should be downstairs."

"Yes, miss."

This was a bit much. *Had I asked for it?* There was something annoying about self-effacing men. Didn't he have a life? Didn't he have anywhere to go? Things to do? Of course, he did.

"Aiden, get down to the shop right now and open up. I'll be there shortly." And he was off down the stairs.

I was loathed to let him upstairs after that, but when I was tired, I would lock up and prop my feet on a crate, and he would sit in front of me and massage them. His hands were so soft they felt like silk against my skin. I would often fall asleep in the chair and wake with a start to send him packing before it got dark.

Every time I vowed I would not succumb to his hands, but time after time I failed. I was fraught with a desire for this pleasure and at the same time a growing disdain for the effeminate nature of his ministrations on my person.

In the meantime, business was growing and thriving. I had time to work at the real joy of my craft while Aiden took up more and more of the busy work and the hard labor. He was even beginning to learn some of the simpler techniques.

One night, Aiden 's hands were not only relaxing but stimulating. They inched up around my ankles, onto my calves, and when his silken fingers reached the back of my knees, I bolted.

"Time to go, Aiden," I said. I slammed the door on the way upstairs and fell on the bed. I was hot and tingling. I could not breathe. I ran a bath, and taking off my underwear, I was appalled at the wetness of my panties. *No. No.* All my dreams of the man I might find were not of weak, feminine Aiden but of the ideal customer, the bold, muscular young men who hung around more and more lately. And yet, my fondness for Aiden seemed to grow.

The next day, I asked for my usual massage. I found that I could not object as he ran his warm fingers all the way up my leg. The part of me that would have pushed him away had faded with the old empty me. I was turned on and wet. My legs were shaking and limp with pleasure.

"Would you like me to continue further, miss?" Aiden asked so simply, as if further were a pat on the shoulder or a shake of the hand.

"Yes, Aiden," I said. "Continue." I was trying to sound firm, acting as if I were in charge. There was no doubt he would do as told, for, in fact, in all the time I had known Aiden he had never disobeyed me. "Continue," I said again with more force.

He did. His hands worked their subtle way into my panties, under them, into my folds with his warm fingers, swirling them around inside me and slathering all the juices about until my thighs were wet with sweet juice. At last, he pulled my panties down from under my skirt, kneeled before me and cleaned me up with his tongue, sweet and small like a cat's, lapping at last at my hardened clit. I was moaning with pleasure. I convulsed and shot more juice onto his face. He paused long enough to look up at me smiling broadly and dripping with my cum all over his mouth.

"Oh, yes, miss," he cooed.

It was not the last time that Aiden pleasured me thus.

Within a few weeks, I began to notice a change in my customer base. More young men were arriving, looking for potions to increase their manliness or to sweeten a young girl's fancy. They stayed longer and looked more directly at me. Some even talked a while before leaving, glancing back over their shoulders with a final smile.

One night before my bath, I looked in the mirror, thinking briefly of my sadness and the girl who was a void, only to find that my face surprised me. My eyes looked brighter, my lips looked fuller. My shape too had begun to fill and curve. I ran my hand over my hips, relishing the smoothness and muscle there. I loosened the bun, threaded my fingers through my hair, and let the tresses fall. How had I developed such soft shining hair? Something wonderful was happening to me.

I attributed my change to the attentions of the young male customers. Soon I began to imagine them asking me out. I fancied them touching me, making love to me, but in the manly way that I longed for—tossing me on a bed and uncovering their hard cocks for my viewing pleasure, mounting me like a stallion and riding me until I cried out for mercy.

## Lovers

Before long, I took a lover, a dandy who hung around asking for potions to make women fall for him. Many times, for many women. *He must be a fine lover,* I thought. His manner was seductive and placating in the shop, but when he got upstairs, he turned into a beast, tossing me on the bed, dragging off my underwear and shoving his hot cock into me. I gave him the benefit of the doubt. Perhaps he thought that was what I wanted, and although his roughness was irritating, I pretended pleasure in it.

It took no more than three times before I grew weary of him. He had no manners when he was alone with me. He liked to have me from behind with his pants still puddled around his shoes and hurry off to who-knew-what other liaison.

I had been sending Aiden away early. He was clearly not my idea of a man of stature or sophistication. Now that I was attractive, there were other options. Emboldened by my newfound beauty, I began flirting, teasing the men who came into the shop and inviting them upstairs for an afternoon of lovemaking. My choices became better over time.

My gentlemen were the finest examples of great muscle and cock. Stallions of the city. A match to my beauty and allure. Eventually, I became known for my afternoon trysts. Suitors would line up at the door and hang around the counter, hoping for a taste of my sweet wine. I thought I was supremely happy.

Aiden minded the shop like a champion, never shirking the work or complaining. Often, he had to knock on the door and ask for instructions—which he was always doing just at the most inopportune moments. I confess to putting him through many scoldings.

Not only did I scold Aiden, but I also became lax in restocking my potions. My mind was constantly on other things. My regular customers began to shy away. I stood at the same mirror once again and looked into my eyes. Dullness was returning to them. My hair once full and glowing had become limp again and hard to manage. The first hint of wrinkles had begun to show in my face.

In dismay, I threw myself even deeper into the lovemaking. After all, this was what made me beautiful, so it must continue to keep me beautiful. My lovers were all just as satisfied with me and did not fail to keep returning. I, on the other hand, began to notice that the pleasure I once took, if indeed it had been what I thought, did not satisfy.

All the while I had been searching for that delicious sensation that was promised by sex, yet finding only the action. The strutting and posturing, the endless pumping and groaning, the spurting release of male semen in my belly. I was filled with the energy of every man who had dumped himself into me. I was more and more turned on and less and less released. The power of sex flooded me and overflowed into my mind, which became agitated and cruel, and into my emotions, which became angry and bitter.

I began to close the door on my lovers, cursing their selfish cravings and secluding myself in the upper room, while Aiden, good boy that he was, minded the shop.

In spite of Aiden's hard work, the shop began to fail. Without the old customer base, without the young men, there were fewer and fewer jangles of the old brass bell on the door. Fewer and fewer coins in the till. I had nothing to pay Aiden, yet he stayed on, scraping the last bits from many jars and tins of ointments and herbs. I had no energy or desire to refill them.

## Reunion

I woke to the sight of Aiden sitting beside me. I had slept fitfully and knew I must smell of night and sweat.

"Go away."

"No, miss."

"Go," I reiterated, with some force. "Or I will fire you."

"You cannot fire me because you have not paid me for weeks, so I do not work for you any longer."

"Then what are you doing here?" My mind was beginning to return to real life.

"Looking after you, miss."

My mind filled with retorts, *I don't need looking after. Who do you think you are coming into my room? Why don't you just leave me alone?* I looked at him.

But before I could open my mouth, I noticed the few grey hairs sweeping up from his forehead. My eyes lingered on the straight, firm nose, ran down to the mouth that had once been wet against my cunt. I could not send him away. We were becoming old together.

He waved a plate of eggs and hot buttered toast past my nose. I found that I still had a sense of smell. And the food smelled good. I sat up in bed and wolfed it down.

He waited for me, watching me chew and swallow, patient and calm as always, not a hint of judgment or anger.

"I can't run the shop alone, miss."

"Then you shouldn't try."

Suddenly all the past weeks tumbled through my brain, and I felt exhausted again. I sagged back onto the pillows.

"Get up and shower and brush your teeth, miss."

He stood and pulled the covers off my body dragging them to the foot and all the way off the end of the bed.

"What do you think you're doing?"

"Helping you, miss."

My irritation was like a fire in my belly. I tugged my disheveled gown down around my knees. But what did that matter? There was nothing he had not seen. So, I flung my legs off the bed and rose, wobbly, to recover the bedclothes, but he was faster than me and pulled them away.

"I'll be downstairs opening the shop," he said, "and I've put a 'FOR SALE' sign in the window. If you're not going to run it and I can't run it, then it's no use keeping it open."

"You did what!"

I almost ran after him but realized nothing could be done about the sign faster than I could shower and dress. I did so, my fury steaming right along with the hot water.

Aiden was with a customer when I arrived in the shop, so the explosion I'd planned was trapped behind my lips. I searched the window for a sign. None to be found. Aiden had tricked me.

While waiting around to exert my anger on Aiden, I began to notice that numerous empty bottles lined the shelves. I checked several tins for their contents, to my dismay. We were sorely out of many goods. I spent a couple of hours in the back room restocking the easiest things and forgot about the ruse of the sign. I slacked off around the lunch hour and sent Aiden out with our last bit of profit to purchase a few supplies that we lacked. The afternoon passed quickly as my magick returned, filling my hands and mind with familiar skills.

I locked the door and turned to Aiden.

"You have saved me, friend," I said. Recognition of my sad state and the loss I would have known without Aiden's intervention settled around me.

He looked down at the floor. "More than a friend," he said. "Lover." He fluttered his eyelashes and gazed up at me, his brown eyes liquid pools.

"Are you crying, Aiden?"

I could not believe my own idiocy. All this time Aiden had been my source of love and beauty, and when I pushed him away, everything had turned. My heart melted right there as if it had been a dish of sherbet, pooling slowly at the bottom of my belly, dripping into my cunt, steady drops of liquid sweetness. I knelt in front of him.

"Forgive me," I cried, wrapping my arms around his hips, nestling my face against his hot sex, caring for it as he had done mine. And under my face, a hot cock began to uncurl, hard and insistent, pressing into my cheek. I undid his pants and freed the most beautiful member I had ever seen, sculpted with the enchanting curves, straining with length and girth, colored with the rainbow of blood and flesh and throbbing blue veins. I stripped him of every piece of clothing. How could I have missed that lean body? Those small but defined abdominals, the roundness of his shoulders and buttocks, the deep plunge of the groin muscles, furred and hot and diving straight down to the magnificent cock. I reached to touch it.

"No, miss," he said putting his hand on mine before it came in contact with the tip of his cock. "You first."

Enthralled, I read the witch's entire story seated on the floor in the empty shop. Night fell outside, and I had lit a small hand lamp in order to continue. My assistant had been with me when we found the bodies. They were practically skeletons by the time anyone noticed. We had shaken our heads at their position on the bed, his head buried into her pelvis. Now I understood, both his desire and mine. I tucked the notebook into my jacket.

The way to my assistant's home was deep dark by now, but I was emboldened by my new understanding. We had the most tempestuous of relationships. She kept trying to run things, and I kept fighting to resist her, but always wanting in the depths of my heart to yield and be ruled. As a man in this world, I could not. But perhaps in the privacy of another world, I might find that pleasure. Perhaps she might find a role with me equally fulfilling.

She would read it for herself. She would realize that I am Aiden.

# The Longer We Wait

Adeline Fox

Tristan Canova was the first person I'd ever met who openly talked to me about bondage. Openly, confidently, and unashamedly, he put into words scenarios which I had only dreamt about, fantasies I would never have otherwise dared to acknowledge aloud to anyone.

Before Tristan, I had partners who would indulge my desires, but that's all it meant to them. They did it for me, not the other way around. If I got the courage to ask a partner to tie me up, for example, they'd do it. But I'm submissive. I wanted a Dom. I needed a Dom, someone to use me as an instrument for pleasure. Someone who got off on my pain, my discomfort, my willingness to do whatever he needed. Someone who would deny me orgasms, tell me when to come, and punish me for disobeying.

Tristan was more than just willing to indulge me. He wanted me to indulge him. He got it, which made things that much sexier.

When he talked about BDSM, he didn't care who was around to hear it. He had no shame. It was sexy just to hear him make a joke, a pun about tying someone up or spanking them. He said these things matter of factly, with a smirk on his handsome face. Once the door to these conversations was opened between us, it never shut.

I'll never forget the first time the subject came out into the open. I was actually the first one to breach the subject, but it was under the guise of a joke, and I never expected it to open up a strange and intoxicating bond between us.

We were in a grocery store, one of the least romantic places imaginable. Fluorescent lights were glaring, registers beeping and cash drawers slamming shut. It was an unpleasant, overstimulating place, a symbol of the mundanity of adulthood which I was only just beginning to become accustomed to as a twenty-one-year-old in her final year of college. Tristan, on the other hand, was twenty-nine, and bitter. He teased me for my incompetence as a shopper, as a cook, as an adult in general. I could barely remember to mail my rent check on time.

We were shopping with Tristan's housemate, Finn. Finn was a conventionally attractive, muscular blonde guy. We often joked about how attractive Finn was, which became an indirect and safe way for us to flirt with one another, without any risk of rejection.

Tristan was just as attractive, and more so if you asked me, but in a less conventional way. He had a head of messy, dark curls which he often had to brush out of his eyes. But his blue eyes were bright, his thin facial features and prominent bone structure sometimes made me tongue tied, even though we had been friends for years.

Finn was a bouncy, energetic person, and he often wandered off in public without telling us where he was going. On this particular occasion, he had darted down some aisle, like a child who'd caught sight of something exciting.

Done with our own shopping, Tristan and I walked quickly around the store, peering down aisles and sighing in frustration at our inability to find Finn.

"We need to put a leash on that boy," Tristan said.

It was an innocent enough comment, something anyone might have said, really. But there was something in his tone which betrayed layers of meaning, whether intentional or not. There was something in his playful and flirtatious cadence that led me to say what I said next.

"I'd like that," I said. I did not dare to make eye contact as I said it. I felt my cheeks flush, a biological reaction I wish I could control, but never can. I pretended to look around the store, for Finn.

"Oh yeah?" Tristan answered. "I'm learning so much about you lately, Zoey."

I laughed, mostly from nervousness, and we found Finn the very moment we stopped looking for him.

We both turned around after we heard Finn say, "What's so funny?"

Finn had a six pack in one hand and a basket of frozen junk food in the other. I wasn't the only adult-in-training at the time. Finn was twenty-three and not much better at taking care of himself than I was at taking care of myself.

"Oh nothing," Tristan said. Not only had we brushed against the topic of bondage, now we had a secret.

I wished Tristan and I were still alone, but the three of us now made our way to the nearest register. I wanted to clarify my joke with Tristan. I didn't completely mean what I had said. At least not the exact way I had said it. It wasn't Finn I wanted, and in any case, I'm the one who wears the leash.

Back at the house, Tristan started cooking, pulling ingredients and spices out of the cabinets in preparation for dinner. The sun was setting outside the window above the sink, the sky becoming a darkening monochromatic blue. It was only four-thirty, in early December, that chaotic period between Thanksgiving and Christmas when, in the life of an English major in college, the reality is nothing but essay writing and intermittent panic. I had to write a paper for each of my five classes—twenty-five pages total due by the end of the week.

For Tristan, and his housemate Finn, this was a week like any other, spent primarily at the bar downtown working ten, twelve-hour shifts. Tristan was a chef and Finn a bartender. If they were lucky, maybe the restaurant would close on Christmas, but there was no long, relaxing break for them to look forward to.

I just had to make it through this week. I should have been at home studying this very moment, not standing in Tristan's kitchen watching the sun set behind him as he systematically lined up ingredients on the small wooden counter.

Tristan rolled his eyes at my stress with the wisdom of someone soon to turn thirty. How soon exactly, I couldn't know. He intentionally avoided talking about his birthday, hoping people would forget that he was a human being capable of aging and even growing old one day.

This reluctance to discuss his exact age only peaked my curiosity, however, making Tristan's birthday a running joke between the three of us. Finn and I wished Tristan a happy birthday daily, hoping to catch something in his demeanor, a tell indicating that we'd hit upon the correct, mysterious date. Tristan had no Facebook page, and remarkably little could be found about him online.

I flipped on the fluorescent overhead light in his dirty kitchen, and he handed me a potato peeler, saying nothing, gesturing to the potatoes on the counter.

Practically as soon as I put the peeler to the skin, Tristan scoffed. He took both of my hands in his, wrapping his body around mine, forcing my fingers and hands into the proper position and movement.

"Got it?" he asked, speaking directly into my ear which was only inches away from his mouth. It was a question, but his tone was more of a command.

Finn went skipping past us down the narrow corridor of the kitchen, which was the size of a small hallway, with barely two feet between the stove and the counter on the opposite side. The walls of the kitchen were painted a baby blue which contrasted with the deep wood of the rest of the house. We had deemed this place The Cabin. I'd been sleeping on the couch for the better part of the past two weeks. Neither Tristan nor Finn seemed to mind at all, and each of them was equally happy to hang out with me on their days off.

I woke up each morning and drank coffee with whichever of them was awake. If pressed I would have had no good explanation as to why I didn't just walk home each night. I lived a two-minute walk around the corner, just over the river. I thought it must be obvious to the boys that I had a crush on at least one of them. Sometimes we even joked about having a threesome, since both of the boys were bisexual. I just hoped that my joking about Finn's attractiveness had not thrown Tristan so far off the trail as to think I wasn't interested in him.

But we were flirting, right?

I can never tell. Seduction is not my strong suit. I guess that's part of why I just want someone else to come along and take the reins, romantically and sexually. If Tristan's commanding nature in the kitchen was any indication, this would not be a problem for him.

"I need a cigarette," Finn said as he walked by. His words were muffled since he already had one between his lips. He pulled it out of his mouth and smiled at us as he opened and closed the back door in one swift motion.

"I want one too," I said, putting down my half-peeled potato. "May I go, boss?" I asked, my arms behind my back, leaning on the counter.

"You wouldn't last a day in a kitchen," he said, but he put down his long knife and headed outside. On the porch, Finn was seated on a filthy plastic chair with his feet on the lowest rung of the fence in front of him. He was using his legs to tip his chair onto its back legs, staring at the stars and blowing gray smoke up into the sky. I sat next to him, ashtray between us. Tristan stood leaning against the fence. Behind him, the river flowed by, reflecting the light of a full moon. We didn't even need the light on the side of the house in order to see, but it had the effect of reflecting the red paint of the house, casting everything in a sinister glow.

Each of us gazed wordlessly at the rushing river beyond the trees.

Between Finn and Tristan's backbreaking jobs and my looming deadlines, each of us could use some relief, preferably in the form of something healthier than tobacco. Tristan would be cooking his signature winter soup, a recipe which he refined in and outside of his workplace, which he was kind enough to share with his friends on cold nights like this one.

I could see the river easily through the trees which had shed most of their leaves. I was shivering, and the boys had finished their cigarettes. I snuffed mine out but balanced it in one of the indentations on the outer ring of the ashtray, for later. I was only an occasional smoker, and it took me longer to finish one.

We made our way back inside. Finn went straight to his room and shut the door while Tristan and I finished preparing dinner. Soon my diligently peeled and chopped potatoes, carrots, and celery were simmering in Tristan's homemade broth.

"Now, we wait," he said.

I leaned back on my heels for a moment, waiting for further instructions. Tristan made a subtle "follow-me" type of gesture, his hand brushing against my arm. I followed him around the corner, through the living room, and down the hall. His bedroom was at the end of a hallway, and strangely enough, was down a small staircase—a set of just three steps.

Tristan's room was cluttered. He simply had a queen-sized bed with layers of messy blankets, and a desk with a computer. Books, papers, dirty boots, and empty—I checked— packages of cigarettes were strewn about everywhere.

I often felt compelled to clean the house, particularly on the days that both boys had work and I hung around waiting for either of them to come home and hang out with me. But most of the trash was seemingly important; bills, pay stubs, receipts lining all the surfaces. The only thing they bothered to keep organized in the house was the growing tower of Domino's pizza boxes, which was now taller than the kitchen counter.

Being left alone in the house, as I was most days, felt almost intimate. The way I was permitted to, in Tristan's words, "stay as long as you want and just lock up whenever you leave," meant that he had trusted me with his personal possessions. Trusted me not to steal anything, not that there was anything worth stealing. Trusted me not to go through his things, trusted me not to read his pay stubs or receipts or pore through his sketchbooks from college, from before he dropped out. And I didn't, either. Even though he never told me not to go through these things, of course, I didn't.

In the living room, I occasionally found coasters from the bar where the boys worked and flipping them over, discovered names and phone numbers written on the back, which made me mildly jealous. But I could never tell which boy they had been given to, and likely they were for Finn, the bartender. The only thing in the house I had read extensively was a book in Tristan's bedroom entitled, *Your Guide to Male Multiple Orgasms*.

It turned out to be less interesting than I thought it would be. I guess I just wanted to get into the male mindset, into Tristan's mindset. I wondered if he were able to reap all that the title had promised.

In his bedroom, Tristan sat on the one chair he had at his desk.

"Shut the door," he said as I walked down the stairs. He wasn't facing me when he said it. He was looking at something on his computer, which he quickly shut. He swiveled his chair to face the center of the room. Since he had taken the only seat available, I sat at the edge of his unmade bed, facing him. Expectant.

He rolled his chair toward me and placed one leg on either side, enclosing me in a V shape. I leaned back onto my hands. Feeling bold, I put my feet on the edge of his chair, dangerously close to him, then leaned forward, and kissed him.

I pulled on his short hair as I did so, and soon he moved up onto the bed and fully wrapped his legs around me. But by that point, he was sitting on top of me, rather awkwardly, and we both burst out into laughter which made it easier to fall back into a more natural, horizontal position on the bed. The moonlight was seeping in through both of his windows in spite of heavy blinds.

"I've wanted to do that for a while," he said.

"Well," I said, wanting to sound casual, trying not to give away my excitement. "Happy birthday then." I hadn't wished him one yet that day. I looked into his eyes, but he maintained a complete poker face. No telling one way or the other. I had known him for more than a year as friends, though it was only recently that I'd started wishing him happy birthdays on a daily basis. Still, his twenty-ninth had come and gone, and I had no idea. His thirtieth could be any day.

"So. Did you mean what you said?" he asked, "about the leash?"

"Hmmm ... What do you think?" I replied.

"I think you're a classic example," he said. "It's always the quiet ones. The ones you'd least suspect. You're filthy," he said, whispering into my ear before nibbling on it so perfectly I couldn't help but sigh.

This was my chance. I wanted to tell him my exact fantasies—all of them, in perfect detail, things I had never told anyone. But that could wait. A little mystery would keep things more exciting. So, I turned my head to face him and said simply, "You can do whatever you want to me. I just want to please you. You don't have to ask. In fact, don't ask."

"Well then we're going to need a safe word," he said.

"Yes. Okay ..." I said, trying to think of something suitably unsexy to use.

"Those aren't very good safe words," he said, joking. "What's something you'd never say in bed?"

"Supercalifragilisticexpialidocious!" I sorta yelled.

"Something with fewer syllables," he said, kissing my neck.

"Pancake," I said.

"Are you sure you'd never say that?" he asked. "Not even as a term of endearment? My little pancake?"

"Gross!" I said.

"Well then it's settled," he said.

Then he shot me a look I'd never seen before. No one had ever looked at me with such an expression. Everything about his demeanor was confident, commanding. His strong, sharp jawline became tight, his light red lips pursed into a sinister smile. There was a glimmer of excitement in his blue eyes.

His face at that moment was just the tiniest bit frightening, or else it would have been frightening if this moment had not been preceded by a lighthearted and important conversation about boundaries.

Instead of frightening me, his face and suddenly taught, clenched muscles sent my heart racing in the best possible way. I was laying on my side at the time, running my hands up and down his, playfully.

Without warning, he pushed me over with the full force of his strength. Now I was flat on my back, staring up at the wooden beams that crisscrossed his white ceiling. He took my wrists in his hands and forced them down into the mattress. Then he used his legs to secure mine open, spread eagle. I tried struggling a little, just for fun, something I had always wanted to do but never had the courage to try before with other partners. I thrashed my head back and forth and tried to force my arms and legs out from under his, but couldn't budge.

He laughed at my attempt to break free, and I could feel his erection through his jeans. He loved watching me struggle.

Tristan was relatively small. His muscles were toned, but not huge. His demeanor when I met him before I peeled back the layers of his personality through flirtation, he was nothing but gregarious and kind. In no way did he seem like the kind of person who would take such unabashed pleasure in restraining a woman while she thrashed and struggled beneath him.

That's not to say I think there's anything shameful about kink. Not at all; it comes from a place of mutual trust and respect. Discovering Tristan's shocking, well-concealed dark side only made things more exciting, surprising, and hot.

I was especially surprised to find that, playing or not, I genuinely couldn't escape his grasp. Even if I used every muscle in my body and fought as hard as I could, he was too strong. Then he pulled both of my wrists together, and amazingly, with just one hand, was still able to hold me down.

This freed up one of his hands to venture up my shirt and pinch one of my nipples so hard that I couldn't help but let out a small yelp. Tristan then took his hand out of my shirt and covered my mouth with it for a moment. I whimpered under his fingers and pleaded "no" with my eyes.

He let me squirm like that for a few seconds, still grinning. Then he took his hand off of my mouth and instead placed it on my crotch. He pushed hard against my jeans. I was so horny that it hurt.

"Do you want me?" he asked, in a flat, unaffected tone.

"Yes!" I said, perhaps a little too loud. I wondered what Finn had heard of our encounter. Then I repeated quieter, in a whisper, "Please." My heart was beating hard now, my breath was coming fast. I kept trying to reach Tristan's face with mine, wanting to kiss him as a way of thanking him for this. But I was too restricted, I could barely move my neck, and he did not lean down to kiss me.

Instead, he brought his mouth to my ear only to say, "Hmmm hmm hmm hmm." His tone was mocking. "I know. Too bad. You have to wait."

I let out a frustrated gasp. I was genuinely shocked. No one had ever done this to me before, and though, admittedly, I had always fantasized about denial and teasing of this magnitude, I didn't expect it to be so disappointing.

I supposed that the reward would come later.

That was the whole point.

He released all of my limbs at once and kissed me, pressing his hard-on against my jeans. He denied himself, too, all in order to tease me. All to torture me into submitting to his every wish and whim, later.

When he finally let me.

Who knows how long he would make me wait.

I ached. I begged for him to please just let me suck his cock, that's all I wanted. He could put it up my ass if he wanted. I promised I wouldn't come. But even with that, he would not allow me.

"Not yet," he said, holding my neck in his hands. As much as I wanted him at that moment, I also wanted to do whatever he said. I trusted him and wanted to obey his words.

"Okay," I said, resigned to wait as long as it took.

"One more thing," he said, once again taking my wrists and holding them down with all of his might, the muscles on his arms glowing in the moonlight. "Call me Sir," he commanded.

"Yes Sir," I said.

I threw my legs around his body, tried to keep him close, but he pulled away. Standing now, he leaned down to kiss me once more.

"Gotta check on the soup!" He said, changing modes completely.

He left me there in his bed. I was surrounded by a lingering smell of light, pleasant cologne. I had never gotten close enough to Tristan to notice it before. It smelled nice.

I followed him to the kitchen where he stood stirring the soup with a big wooden spoon. I wrapped my arms around his stomach and rested my head on his shoulder.

Finn emerged from his bedroom, wearing pajamas now. I felt at home in this house with my soon-to-be lover and our mutual friend. The soup was steaming on the stove, and I felt warm, inside and out. My disappointment and frustration quickly gave way to contentment. There was still so much to look forward to.

"Is dinner ready yet?" Finn asked. He made no comments about my affectionate stance leaning against Tristan. It could not have come as much of a surprise to him, having watched me pine and flirt for weeks, likely catching me looking at Tristan whenever I thought he wouldn't notice me doing so.

"Not yet," Tristan said. "It'll taste better the longer we wait."

The three of us played cards around the kitchen table for an hour until the soup was deemed ready. Then the three of us gathered on the futon with steaming bowls of soup and mugs of Cabernet Sauvignon. The boys did not own wine glasses, and for once I had a chance to lightheartedly scold Tristan for his lack of adult housewares.

"Well, I don't drink wine," he said.

"Then why'd you buy it?" I asked.

"You like wine," he said, then he kissed my forehead.

"Okay. I wasn't gonna say anything," Finn said, "But you guys are making me a little sick with your affection. I'm trying to enjoy my dinner."

"Gee, Finn." Tristan said, "You're welcome. No, it was really no trouble making you dinner."

After dinner, I retreated to Tristan's bedroom. He returned to his commanding mode, everything about his demeanor changing the instant he shut the door behind us. This time, he locked it.

I stood a few feet away from him, hands behind my back, awaiting instruction. His hands deftly unhooked his belt and slid it out of the loops on his jeans. I took a deep breath in anticipation, hoping I'd finally get to see his cock. I almost knelt to my knees right there but instead waited.

Instead of tossing the belt aside, though, he pulled it on both ends—snapping it at eye level to me. Then he made a loop with it and held it in his dominant hand. I wondered what he was going to do next.

He exhaled. "Bend over the desk," he said, very slowly. Calmly.

I scoffed a little, out of nerves.

"Now," he commanded.

I did as I was told, feeling completely vulnerable, staring at the grey wall ahead of me. I couldn't see him at this angle, but I could feel the heat of his body behind mine.

"Slide your arms to the edge of the desk," he said. "And hold on. Tight."

I did exactly as he told me, white-knuckled.

He leaned over me and whispered, once again, into my ear.

"We need to talk about punishment," he said. Then he pulled my skirt and tights down, exposing my ass. I could feel him backing away from me. He slapped the belt against his hand once. Twice. Three times. I tensed up every time I heard the leather hitting his skin.

"I'm going to need you to be honest with me," he said. "I need to know how to punish you. So, starting off easy ... tell me ... how does this feel?"

He hit me with the belt, and I let out a short moan.

"Good," I admitted.

"That won't do," he said. "How about this?"

He hit me harder. The belt made a loud smack as it made contact with my skin.

"That hurt," I said.

He did it again, just as hard.

"How much?" He asked.

"A lot," I said, grabbing tightly to the edge of his desk.

"I think you can take more," he said, hitting me just once, with much greater force than any of the previous times. I whimpered but did not move or use the safe word. I heard him throw the belt onto the bed, but I did not turn around or ask him what he planned to do next. The mystery was intoxicating. I felt the heat of the pain on my ass warming my whole body.

I heard a drawer open, then Tristan's footsteps walking back toward me.

"Now," he said. "That's just what you'll get if you disobey me. For small disobedience. If you forget to call me Sir. If I tell you not to move or flinch and you do. But for bigger transgressions ..."

I heard a cap opening. He was pouring lotion or lube on something.

"Like coming without asking, or worse, coming after I expressly tell you not to. Then you're gonna get my cock up your ass. But you haven't earned the right to feel my cock yet, so just for practice ..."

I felt one of his hands on my hip. He pushed me back down onto the desk and pulled on my hair. Then he slid a dildo up my ass.

"We'll try this," he said. "How does it feel?"

He was kind enough to use lube, but still, it was big. Once he slid the tip in, he forced the rest in, quickly. Hard. I yelped. He laughed.

"It hurts," I said.

"But do you like it?" he asked.

I squirmed a little.

"No," I said. "But I'll take it for you."

"Perfect. We've found our punishment. And with that, you're ready." He slid the dildo out.

He commanded me to stand upright, and pulled me by the arm, over to the bed. He undressed me. He put my arms and legs in spreader bars. I was stuck, vulnerable, spread-eagle on his bed. I begged for him to touch me. He undressed himself by the side of the bed, leaving me waiting. He said nothing as I begged. I'd been wet ever since the belt hit my skin. I'd been aching ever since he teased me hours before. I'd been fantasizing since our conversation in the grocery store.

No one had ever denied me like this. When Tristan did speak, it was only to tell me, "No, not yet." Instead, he slapped my face, commanded me to, "Open," and shoved his cock into my mouth. With my hands to my sides stuck in cold, metal restraints, and Tristan's folded legs on either side of my neck, I was completely trapped. I had no choice. He shoved himself down my throat. We both moaned. I slid my tongue all around his cock, closing my eyes in complete bliss, doing my best to please him. With the small range of motion I was allowed, I reached my neck up to get his cock as far down my throat as I could.

He made me suck him, as a form of teasing, for what felt like an eternity. Eventually, he reached his hand behind him and gently touched my clit, just enough to send shivers up my spine and set my legs shaking with desire. He moaned, and occasionally laughed as he touched me ever-so-gently, seeming to gain just as much pleasure from teasing me as he did from having his cock in my mouth. He would rub my clit until I moaned heavily, then stop. Then, waiting a few minutes, start over again. I pleaded as best I could with his cock in my mouth.

Finally, he took it out. I gasped for air, my breath short from the excitement.

"I think you've earned a reward," he said. He lay across my spread-open body, holding his cock in his hand. He slid over my clit and pussy but wouldn't put it in. I pleaded.

"You want me to fuck you?" He asked. His tone, once again, was utterly unaffected. Like he could care less. Teasing.

We were face to face now.

"Please please please," I said.

"Please what?" he asked, slapping the side of my ass.

"Please. Sir."

"Good girl," he said, and finally, he slid his cock inside me. I practically could have come right then, but I knew he wouldn't let me. He swiveled his hips, hitting my clit just how I like. His expression was confident. He knew how much I loved this. He knew how good he was at this. I moved against him as best I could, but my movement was restrained. I felt so free, letting him fuck me just how he wanted.

"Thank you, Sir," I said. I meant it. I was so grateful.

But the games weren't over yet.

"Can I come?" I asked.

He laughed again. "So soon?" He said. "I should spank you just for asking. But you'll learn."

I moaned and whimpered, exerting as much restraint as I could muster not to come. There was no way I'd be able to come without him noticing, it would be monumental when it happened, and I'd likely be unable to control myself, my volume, my obvious spike in pleasure. Plus, I wanted to obey. I loved seeing his face full of bliss and gratification.

Then I learned something remarkable about Tristan. I watched his face distort in gorgeous pleasure and felt him come inside me. His body rippled toward me, fucking me hard, groaning loudly.

I couldn't believe it. He wasn't going to let me come at all! I couldn't take this anymore. I'd have to jerk off in the bathroom after he fell asleep. There was no way I'd be able to fall asleep feeling so horny.

But I couldn't betray his trust like that.

In any case, he didn't stop fucking me when we came.

I remembered the book in his room, the one about multiple orgasms. I didn't even know it was possible, but he didn't lose his erection.

But he didn't let me come either. Instead, he flipped me over and fucked me in the ass for several minutes as punishment for daring to ask if I could come.

I felt a hot, sharp pain, mixed with extreme pleasure. I felt Tristan's hot breath warming my neck as he moaned against me.

"Take it," he said, and I did. I took it for him, and amidst extreme pain, I grew even wetter listening to him moaning behind me. I loved it, loved being the source of his pleasure, being able to take such pain for him. I felt strong, tough, desirable. Feeling his body against my back made me feel warm, even safe, in spite of the pain.

He forced me to say things, something else I'd always fantasized about but never experienced.

"Tell me you love it," he'd command. I struggled to get the words out amidst my whimpers, moans, and sharp, pained breaths. If I refused to say it, he explained, he'd only fuck me harder.

"Say you love my cock in your ass. Say you're a bad girl who doesn't deserve to come."

It would utterly humiliate me for anyone to know I'd said such things or further that I enjoyed saying them. Then again, that was part of the fun.

Fucking my ass, he came, again, and I wondered if he'd make me wait days, weeks, years before he let me have an orgasm.

Still restrained and facing the wall, I wondered what would happen next, if anything. I dreaded the thought of having to wait any longer.

I could feel Tristan moving down to the edge of the bed and wondered why. Then I heard him releasing my legs, then my arms, from the restraints. He set them aside, and flipped me over, giving me a passionate kiss. He thanked me for being so good. He ran his hands all over my body, spread open my legs, moved down the bed and put his lips on my clit. I held his head with both hands, caressing his soft hair, grateful for every lick and pulsation of his pretty lips against me. He looked up occasionally, stopping, one last form of gentle teasing, but a romantic kind this time. This let me see his beautiful, happy, sated face.

"You can come now, beautiful," he said.

And with his lips against my clit, I obeyed his final command.

After I came, holding Tristan's gorgeous face in both my hands and moaning with abandon, he held me, and we cuddled for over an hour. We talked through what we had done, Tristan ensuring that I had an enjoyable time and reminding me that I should use the safe word without hesitation if I were ever uncomfortable at all.

I fell asleep suddenly and woke without any memory of having fallen asleep. But I had slept deeply, soundly, for longer than I usually do, and woke up happy. I was disappointed to find that Tristan wasn't in bed with me, but minutes after I awoke he returned to the room, with pancakes.

"Pancakes for my pancake," he said.

"I told you that was a gross pet-name," I said, but I grabbed a plate, kissed him and thanked him. "Yesterday was amazing," I continued.

"Tell me about it," he said. "I've never had a better birthday."

# Contributors

*Adeline Fox*

Adeline Fox is an educator living in Western Massachusetts. Her work has appeared in Psymposia magazine.

*Gina Durden*

Carolina girl transplanted West who brought the South with her in the form of sensuousness and curiosity. We are all submissive to our fate, to our loves, to our art—unless we create something beyond.

She writes to explore the worlds she cannot inhabit, to search for understanding, to experience the wonder and diversity of all forms of love.